A Valentine's Bind

Bind

A novello

by

Scarlett Flame

To Tracey
with love n Stuff
Scarlett
Flame
x x
x

COPYRIGHT PAGE

DEDICATION

*For my fabulous Street Team Emma Lou Hopkins,
Alison Hucker and Natalie Masters
Thanks for all your help..*

Chapter One

Nicky

I woke up slowly. Opening first one eye then the other tentatively. My head banging and my mouth felt like the bottom of a parrot cage. The need for food immediate and overpowering. The mantra in my head repeating over and over. *I am never drinking red wine again. I am never drinking red wine again.* Then, I spotted the open packets and containers of food spread across the coffee table in the living room. No wonder my neck hurt so much. Falling asleep on the sofa with my head at an unnatural angle will do that to a person.

With a selection of leftovers heated up I began munching aimlessly. Trying to remember how I got home the previous evening. And, the twenty dollar question was "Who with?" I could hear someone coming through my front door with a key. But, I lived alone, and no one else had keys to my flat. Not even my family.

I turned to look as the handle started to twisted, panicking as the door pushed open and in stepped a stunning man with dark brown hair. He was wearing, what looked to me like a Saville Row suit. His steely blue gaze connecting with my own slightly bloodshot pale blue eyes.

Oh. Finally awake are we?" he remarked in a

clipped accent as he walked in shutting the door carefully behind him.

I attempted to swallow the mouthful of curry I was in the middle of chewing and began to cough violently. It had gone down the wrong hole and I was turning an unattractive blue hue.

Reacting quickly he shot over and banged me on the back sharply three times dislodging the errant bit of curry. Which promptly shot out of my mouth, landing on the rug. *Oh. My God. How embarrassing* I didn't have a clue who he was and this is how he gets his first glimpse of me. Eating warmed up curry. Looking like I had been dragged backwards through a hedge. Except, apparently this wasn't our first meeting at all. He had a key to my flat and seemed to know his way around.

What on earth went on last night?

Grabbing some tissues I cleaned up the mess on the rug and guiltily started to tidy up the living area. He grabbed my arm firmly, turned me to face him and commanded.

"Stop that right now. We need to talk. Sit down there."

He pointed to the sofa and I felt an overwhelming compulsion to follow his orders.

"Right. Tell me what you remember from last night. The truth mind you. I won't be lied to."

I opened my mouth, then closed it again. This happened a few times as I had no idea what did happen, how he came to have a key or even how I got home.

"Enough of that now. You look like a demented goldfish, opening and closing your mouth like that. So.

A Valentine's Bind

I assume from your body language and failure to respond that you haven't a clue who I am. No idea what I am doing here or even aware of the fact I had to escort you home."

I nodded and shrugged. Not trusting myself to talk without making the situation worse. So. The "who" I came home with was revealed.

"Well then. Perhaps introductions are in order. For starters I know a little about you already. Your name is Nicola Johnson, or Nicky to your friends. You are a student at Salford University studying sociology, who works in a bar in town part-time. Your parents live in Spain having retired recently. Are you sure you can't remember anything about yesterday evening?" He Quizzed. A stern look on his face.

I stared at him and tried my absolute best to remember something, anything. He did look familiar but I couldn't even remember his name, where we had met or what had led to us coming home together. He wasn't even my type, which was the big shocker. He looked way to sophisticated for a piss poor student like me to snaffle.

"Well...I remember your face. But, other than that it is hazy. I must have drunk way too much red wine last night to blank out the entire evening like this." I replied.

"Oh, petal I think the shots might have something to do with the memory loss. That, and the spliff I found you sharing with the guys that wanted to take you home with them. For a threesome as I remember rightly."

Shocked once again in to silence I began to get brief flashbacks of the previous evening. Again performing my goldfish impersonation. Whoever this person in front of me was, he seemed to have my best interests at heart.

"Erm, yeah I seem to remember a little bit of that happening. I am so sorry. That isn't how I usually behave at all. Please don't tell anyone what happened. I promise that I have learned my lesson and won't do that again."

"Oh. I know you won't. We had a long conversation last night about your behaviour. Your very bratty behaviour I might add. My name, seeing as how your memory has failed you, is Dariel but you will call me Sir. We met in a club by the way. I don't suppose you remember what type of club we met in. Do you?"

This time I shook my head. But, then I had an epiphany and began to remember a little more about the previous evening. I groaned out loud at the revelation. I had gone with some friends from Uni on a night out and we had decided to visit a club after a few too many drinks. A BDSM club to be precise.

"Is that a look of enlightenment, or one of horror I see on your face petal?" he smirked.

"I remember some friends from Uni and I thought it would be a good idea to visit a BDSM club." I answered falteringly. "We had all watched a programme on the telly earlier in the week and it … sort of… looked interesting."

"Hmm. Interesting." he reflected. "Well you certainly bit off more than you could chew last night. Didn't you? You came in shouting that you needed a Dom to take control of you. Instead you acquired the attention of a group of guys that had wandered in off the street, on a stag party."

A Valentine's Bind

Mortified at this latest revelation I dropped my eyes to the floor, counting myself a very lucky girl indeed, to have escaped a fate worse than death.

"Good girl. THAT is why I saw potential in you last night. The fact that you were so biddable and compliant. Your submissive side was very evident or I wouldn't have agreed so readily to our arrangement."

At this I looked up instantly.

"Arrangement?" I stammered. "What arrangement? I have no clue what you mean."

Then, it hit me like a freight train. I finally remembered part of the discussion from the previous evening. Dariel was a Dominant, and he had agreed to my being "under consideration" to become his submissive. Apparently "under consideration" meant that I was his submissive, or a trainee submissive of sorts.

Bile rose in my throat, I stood, then shot off to the bathroom. It seems he took his new position seriously as he followed me quickly. He held my hair back as I swiftly deposited my recently consumed curry down the toilet. I felt a little better once I had finished puking what felt like the entire contents of my stomach. Amazed that Dariel had no problem caring for me. Even managing to find a clean wash cloth and gently wiping my face. Helping me to get off the floor, led me to my bedroom and sat me on the edge of the bed then carefully began to undress me. At first I offered no resistance. Then, I grabbed at his hands and he stopped stock still. Visibly irked.

"Do you have a problem Nicky? He enquired. "Because if not I suggest that you remove your hands now. My patience is not endless. When I tell you to do something it is not a request. It is an order and I expect complete obedience or there will be consequences. Be assured I don't take disobedience lightly."

I looked up into his eyes and could not meet them head on, and let go. Yielding, I allowed him to remove the rest of my clothes with no argument. Which he proceeded to fold neatly and place on the bed. I just kowtowed to him without a struggle. He had such an aura about him that shouted out alpha male.

CHAPTER TWO

Nicky

Once undressed I watched him disappear into the bathroom and heard the shower turn on. He returned and bid me follow. I had my arms over my body trying in vain to cover my nakedness as much as possible. He ushered me under the falling water. I stood there clueless. Should I start to wash myself? I wasn't sure of anything now. Did I need a command to do that? That was when I was aware he had returned, after leaving me briefly alone. Now buck naked. My eyes gravitated of their own accord to the sight of his more than ample engorged cock. Jutting proudly to attention. My mouth watered as I gulped audibly. *How big?* I thought

He stepped into the shower, picking up the soap I watched in nervous anticipation as he began to rub the soap forming a lather. That simple action causing my body to respond. Nipples hardened as he took the loofah and abraded my skin. Petting, pinching and pulling at my nipples until I felt myself flood with

6

moisture. Stimulating my senses, increasing my arousal as he ruthlessly played with my body. Leaving me breathless. Intimately cleaning every part of me. My groans and moans becoming increasingly loud. Unable to hide how turned on I was.

It was the most erotic experience I had ever had. I had never bathed or showered with anyone before unless you counted shared bath times as a child. His questing fingers touching me intimately. His hands gliding deliciously over every curve and contour. He turned me around and began to shampoo my hair. His fingers kneading my scalp firmly. Rinsing the suds away he then used conditioner. Slipping it through my hair and then his fingers followed down to my waist Not content with that he began to massage my rump with skillful strong hands. I could feel his hard on. Hot and throbbing as it brushed again me when he came close.

Once he was happy that I was clean and clearly aroused he began to lather up his own body. I watched appreciatively for a few moments as he began to stroke himself from root to tip. I looked up and was caught in his gaze, mesmerised. I tentatively reached toward him and he nodded his assent. I took over using the lather moving my hands up and over his cock and balls. Weighing his balls gently in my hands. My legs trembling. My heart beating a crescendo in my chest. Dariel took down the shower head then began rinsing the suds from my body and his own. Directing it toward my pussy a little more than necessary.

A Valentine's Bind

Suddenly he grabbed my wrists and held my hands above my head. Pinning me against the tiled wall. His other hand had my throat. Not that hard that it hurt or I couldn't breathe but hard enough this I knew who was in charge. His piercing gaze held me in thrall as I let out a breathy moan. Transfixed, immobile and in torment from my own growing passion. Feeling my core gush and my juices trickle down my inner thigh.

We remained this way for less than a minute but it felt like time had stood still.

"You are mine now." He insisted. "... to do with what I will without question. First though we will discuss your limits. Both hard and soft and agree safe words. For now we will use the traffic light system. Red is stop. Amber is "take a moment", and green is good to go. Nod if you understand me."

I nodded . This action didn't stop my arousal, far from it.

"Good girl" he praised.

In one move his hand left my throat, reached under my bottom lifting my body up. Pushing forcefully into me in one fell swoop. Slamming me against the tiled walls as I instinctively wrapped my legs around him. His cock filling me. Pinching a little but the pleasure outweighed the pain. He smiled ever so slightly as he drove into me again and again. Balls deep his cock pushing forcefully nudging my cervix. Never before had I experienced anything so intense. Stretching me as he continued to ram into me. Claiming me, ruthlessly. His fingers gripping me so

A Valentine's Bind

hard I knew I would have bruises to remind me of this coupling. I felt myself grow hot, my climax approaching.

"Cum for me Nicky. Come for your Sir." he ordered.

I screamed out his name as I exploded.

He continued to hammer into me. His cock growing as the contractions from my pussy pulsated. His hot sperm spurt forth. Filling me up. Not stopping but driving into me.

Only then did I realise we hadn't used any protection whatsoever. What was I thinking?

He continued to thrust into me groaning out his release until we both stilled. Only the automatic responses of our bodies continuing as his cock twitched and my pussy pulsed and spasm around him. Letting my legs uncurl I dropped them to the floor. Unable to hold me up, my legs began to fold but he held me fast. Enveloping me in his arms, nuzzling and kissing my neck.

Turning off the shower and picking me up easily, he pulled me close. Carrying me carefully he stood me up in the bedroom and wrapped a towel around me. Gently patting me dry before he proceeded to dry himself.

Once we were both dried to his satisfaction he climbed in to the bed and held the covers back,commanding me to join him. My head on his chest. Listening to the his heart beat, strong and steady. Lulling me to sleep.

CHAPTER THREE

Nicky

I woke up later that day as dusk was falling. Alone. Tucked up in bed with the blankets swaddled around me. Trying to get my bearings.

Had I imagined all that? Was it all in my head? Dreams? Wet ones for God's sake?

Slowly I began to sit up and felt a gush from my tender pussy.

Oh no! That certainly wasn't my imagination.

Grabbing my dressing gown off the end of the bed I made my way to the bathroom. I needed to pee and clean myself up a little.

I expected the flat to be empty but as I walked through to the living room I stopped and looked around astonished. Hearing noises I continued on toward the little galley kitchen in stunned amazement. Dariel was just putting away the last of the cutlery. My flat was spotless. Turning he leaned against the counter top, cocking his head slightly and queried.

"Good evening Nicky. Feeling better after your

sleep I hope?"

"Yes thank you." I muttered back quietly.

"Yes thank you what? Little sub." he demanded.

"Yes thank you I feel much better." I responded a little louder, confused.

"Yes thank you SIR. You mean." he stated. "Go and shower and get dressed quickly. We are going out for some dinner now and then on to my club. I will choose an outfit for you while you shower."

He walked toward me then placed his hand on the small of my back and pushed me gently but firmly back towards the bedroom where I obediently showered. He had selected a dress from my meagre selection in my wardrobe and it was laid neatly on the bed. My blue suede shoes placed on the floor nearby. Picking up the dress I spotted no underwear so I turned, heading to the small chest of drawers when I heard a tutting from behind me.

"What do you think you are doing Petal? I told you that I would choose what you wear. Which I have. If I wanted you to have panties or a bra they would have been set out on the bed for you. I expect my submissive to be available to me at all times. Therefore, unless I request it, it will be a given that you no longer wear underwear."

"You have got to be joking." I stuttered angrily. " I can't go out without at the very least a pair of panties on."

"You forget your place little sub. This is not a request, but an order. One I expect you to obey. You will speak only with permission. and you will address me as Sir at all times. From now on you are also not allowed to climax without my express permission either."

Ignoring him I opened the drawer and started to rifle through it, grabbing a pair of panties as I did. Sensing a movement behind me I was quickly ensnared by strong arms. The next thing I knew I was face down, flipped over his lap.

"I warned you last night that my patience was not endless, and was growing thin." he added calmly.

Starting to kick and squirm but to no avail as he moved my hands and clasped them behind my back in one swift move. His right leg pinned my own legs in place.

"Oh, little girl you will learn to obey me or suffer the consequences. I am now going to spank your arse until it is the same shade as your hair – red. When I have finished you are going to thank me nicely and address me as Sir or the punishment will start afresh." he dictated.

As he finished talking he lifted up my dressing gown and began to rub my bottom. Sending waves of heat to my face and elsewhere. The first spanks caught me by surprise. Until then I thought he wouldn't go through with his threat.

How wrong could I be I thought.

The spanks got harder and harder . Tears welled in my eyes as I tried to catch my breath. My bottom on fire. I started to fight free again but this time he held me tighter, like a vice. Despite the pain and intense heat what shocked me the most was that my whole body felt aflame. Pussy clenching and dripping in response.

As suddenly as it started the spanking stopped. He began to massage and caress my glowing bottom. This time I couldn't prevent the moans that escaped my lips.

"Well my sweet little sub, have you something that you would like to say to me?" He enquired.

"Thank you Sir." I whispered with a little sob.

"Sorry. I couldn't quite hear you. Did you say something?" He asked.

He continued to pummel my rump and I groaned out loud, shamelessly.

"Thank you Sir." I gasped a little louder.

"Good girl." He responded and those two words made me gush.

Almost as if he could read my mind. Although, I suspect it was my body he could read. His fingers dipped toward my apex as he demanded.

"Open your legs wider for me little sub. I want access to what is mine. The answer I expect is "Yes Sir." and an immediate response or your punishment will begin again."

My legs opened of their own accord and I heard myself respond. "Yes Sir."

He quickly pushed two fingers into me. Stretching me, plunging them in and out. He grunted satisfied with my wanton reaction as I tried to grind against his fingers.

"See. Your body knows what it wants better than you do little sub. Your body is mine to do with as I please. This is the beginning of a journey. A journey where I push your barriers until they are no longer there. Your body will learn to love what we do and the orgasms you experience will take you to heights you never imagined. Your responses please me very much. My good girl."

He continued to stroke my bottom soothingly and then I felt him kiss both cheeks before he released me from his iron grip.

"Up you get. Dress quickly. The sight of your beautiful pink ass has given me quite the appetite."

He helped me to rise and with no further argument I put on the dress and shoes.

"Do you need to use the bathroom before we head out?" He asked. "Leave the door open. Remember your body is mine in all respects. No need for false modesty."

"Yes Sir." I replied nodding my head.

I relieved myself quickly and wiped the evidence of my arousal. The last thing I needed was the embarrassment of a damp patch when I sat down. Dariel still hadn't given me back my key. I didn't expect him to now. He ushered me out the door. Checking the windows were locked before securing the door and pocketing the key.

Taking my hand he led the way downstairs to the main entrance of the building. Once outside he led the way to a sleek black Mercedes parked at the kerb. The sound of the electronic locks letting me know for certain that this was his as he proceeded to open the door for me. Once he was happy that I was

A Valentine's Bind

safely ensconced with my seatbelt fastened, he went around and got in himself.

CHAPTER FOUR

Nicky

We headed on into Manchester and pulled up outside a swish restaurant called "*The Ivy*". I had walked past it a few times, but it was way above my price range. Again Dariel walked to my door, opened it and held out his hand. As there were a few people on the pavement I tried to swing my legs out and around. Gingerly I moved forward concious of my lack of underwear and sore, probably red cheeks.

I could see he was loving my anxiety. A broad smile on his face showing dimples in either cheek.

Who knew a Dom could smile I pondered.

I couldn't help but smile despite my situation. The door was opened as we approached and the *Maître D* appeared as if by magic, greeted Dariel by name and promptly escorted us to a small secluded booth. Dariel had reserved it earlier and I gathered it was his usual booth.

The waiter brought menu's but Dariel took mine off me saying.

A Valentine's Bind

" I will order for you sweet sub. Something healthy after the rubbish you consumed last night. From now on I will order your food. I cleared out your fridge and cupboards earlier as you slept. We can order online and sort out your diet. A Dominant takes care of your body and mind petal."

I responded "Thank you Sir."

I tried to compute what he had just told me about my food. I wondered what, if anything he had left me to eat at all.

Lettuce and rabbit food from now on maybe?

"Good girl. You're learning fast." he remarked.

What was it with those two little words. I felt my core clench again when he said them. What gives?

The wine waiter appeared to take our order and Dariel ordered a bottle of sparkling water, two glasses, ice and lemon. I looked quizzically at him and he started to speak softly.

"In the world of BDSM and the Lifestyle you will find that we do not consume alcohol before playing. Drink can adversely affect pain receptors. Therefore, we will only ever drink after we finish playing little girl. Do you understand?"

I nodded and said "Yes Sir."

"Also. I will never punish with you in anger. Punishments are carried out in order for you to learn. They can also act as a reward as you experienced earlier. Pain and pleasure go hand in glove in our world."

We sat and chatted through dinner. Despite our differences, funnily enough, we had a lot of interests in common. Dariel had ordered steak, new potatoes and salad. With olives as a starter. One of my absolute favourite meals.

I began to relax a little and feel at ease. Almost forgetting my lack of underwear. That was until I felt his hand on my knee. I jumped a little as he began to slide his hand up under my dress and reached the petals of my labia now drenched once more.

Why was this stuff turning me on? I was sat in a restaurant where people could see.

My eyes widened, staring straight ahead, off in to the distance.

"Look at me petal. I want to watch those beautiful eyes."

The connection between us electric. Swiping his fingers through my slick folds, he circled my nub pressing a little harder. Smiling he watched me closely. His fingers wet from my juices beginning to circle my clit. He leaned into me biting my neck. Sending a frisson of heat through my body. My cheeks flushed as heat shot through me like wildfire.

"Open wider sweet sub. I want access to what is mine."

I did what I was told. Willingly. Parting my legs and when he raised an eyebrow, opened up a little more. He continued to tease my now swollen nub and sodden pussy. My breath coming in short gasps, heart rate escalating as the waiter returned to clear away the plates. Never stopping he continued to watch my face. As the waiter turned to walk away he uttered.

"Cum for me my good girl."

A Valentine's Bind

I groaned and rode his hand, biting my lip attempting to stop any noise. Shuddering my release on cue. His fingers never faltered, just carried right on. Gasping and moaning as once again I bucked against his fingers, wringing a further explosive orgasm. Quivering and mewling, bringing my hand to my mouth biting the heel of my hand. My thighs twitched from the effort I was making not to show any outward signs of my release.

"So beautiful and responsive. You enjoyed that despite your misgivings didn't you little sub." he marvelled.

I nodded.

"I didn't hear you petal" he chuckled.

"Yes Sir." I whispered hoarsely."

As my orgasm began to ebb he finally removed his fingers. Bringing them to his mouth. Licking and sucking them greedily and meticulously clean.

"Hmm you taste so sweet I can't wait to eat you out."

He asked for the bill to be put on his account, then rose. I stood on wobbly legs like a new born lamb. He graciously held my elbow. Guiding me across the pavement to the kerb.

CHAPTER FIVE

Dariel

I had no idea this little kitten could be so responsive.

Dazzling indeed. The pupils of her eyes almost wiping out the blue as she had those magnificent multiple orgasms. An exhibitionist who gets aroused by public play. Who knew? She took to the spanking like a duck to water. Colouring up beautifully. I can't wait to take her further, push some boundaries and leave my marks on her.

Welts on that pert derrière would show others who owned her.

I shouldn't have judged her too soon.

Sometimes it is the least likely of people that take up the most unexpected roles. Someone who yields power may also have a deep need to relinquish that power elsewhere, perhaps in the bedroom. The total bitch at work who rules with a rod of iron may well long to kneel naked at a Master's feet.

The relationships of Master/slave and Dominant and submissive are also varied. The depth and feelings involved vast and more complex than vanilla relationships.

A Valentine's Bind

Take me for example. I am Dominant in all spheres of my life and work.

I take command in every situation.

CHAPTER SIX

Nicky

Once again Sir, (as I was now beginning to think of him), took meticulous care of me. Helping me into the car as we set off to another destination. He referred to it earlier as "his club".

Could this be the club we met at last night? I thought *Surely that was in the centre of town but we seemed to be heading out to the industrial area on the outskirts of Manchester.*

At first, I thought maybe he had taken a wrong turn. Or, this was a short cut, but soon we turned off the main road and entered a private car park. A mixture of prestigious and run of the mill cars were dotted about. The area well lit and cameras visible. Adjacent to the exit for the car park was a large industrial unit. Flashing coloured lights visible through the high windows. It could have been any private nightclub or rave for that matter and I could see no signs to advertise what the club was called.

Once we had alighted he took my hand as we

A Valentine's Bind

stepped forward. Other cars arriving more frequently , most people carried holdalls, wearing long coats over their attire. I people watched out of interest wondering what was happening when Sir spoke out loud.

"I can see you are curious about other patrons. A lot of people in the Lifestyle try and keep a low profile so arrive in normal dress and change into their fetish clothing in the changing rooms provided. Some of these patrons are doctors, police, nurses, accountants and quite a few engineers. Never judge a book by it's cover petal."

A few shouted greeting to Sir and he responded easily.

A man dressed all in leather from head to foot was one such acquaintance. With leather pants, waistcoat and black biker leather knee high boots. He had on a long leather trench-coat aka Matrix style. That wasn't what caught my eye though. His companion did. Although it was Winter and Christmas was only a couple of weeks previous the woman he was with was wearing hardly a stitch.

It wasn't obvious as they arrived, as the car had dark tinted windows but as soon as the door opened, the interior illuminated. I gasped. Naked apart from black stockings and suspenders, and wearing a pair of the highest heels I had ever seen. She tottered gracefully forth. As they got closer I looked in astonishment. Her nipples were pierced, chain joining them, draped down over her stomach. Around her neck was a collar with metal spikes and attached to a

A Valentine's Bind

ring at the front was a leash. She had short spiky blonde hair in a bob and was stunning.

The guy was tall. About six foot four and built like a bodybuilder. His nose pierced and he had short, black, spiky hair, with a goatee.

They both gave a little wave as they passed, acknowledging Sir and entered the club.

Dariel was waiting patiently watching my intrigue. I now realised I had stopped walking to take in their appearance.

"What did you think of his slave my pet? Beautiful isn't she? I can't wait until the time comes, and I will bring you here attired similar."

I realised he was studying me closely to see what reaction he got as I tried to retain an air of indifference. He laughed softly when he realised rather than feigned indifference, I was dumbstruck.

I swallowed and wondered when my mouth became so dry? I swear someone had filled my mouth with ashes or sawdust. Swallowing a few times before I could find my voice.

"She is very beautiful Sir. I doubt that would be able to stand in those heels, let alone walk in them. Would you really take me out wearing so little clothing? I think I would die of embarrassment."

"Actually she was a little overdressed for my tastes petal. You will eventually wear nothing but your piercings, collar and heels. You will practice walking in heels until you have accommodated to walking in some possibly baller shoes. I am certain you would look even more delectable dressed that

A Valentine's Bind

way. We will be attending events termed CMnf. Clothed male, naked female. I will of course be suited and booted and you will kneel naked at my feet. You don't look convinced little girl." He insisted. "Be assured it will happen. We are in our incipient stage now. You are a beginner and have a lot to learn. As your Dom I will help to mould you, push and nurture you."

With that he placed his hand on the small of my back and we continued on. My thoughts were chaotic.

Did he really mean all that or was he just trying to intimidate me? Would he truly expect me to accompany him naked to functions? And all that talk about piercings. I almost fainted clean away when I had my ears pierced. Surely he wasn't expecting me to get my nipples pierced?

I absent-mindedly touched my nipples through my dress.

Ouch. Surely not. I wondered.

I hadn't even realised we had got to the doorway until he once again spoke. Pulling me to one side gently.

"Petal. Before we enter my club there are a few rules you need to obey." clicking his fingers to catch my attention. "Earth to Nicky. What planet are you on? Now, listen and absorb, as this is important. Because you aren't wearing a collar other Doms may show interest in you. As this marks you as available. You will stay close to me and keep your eyes downcast at all times. No wandering off on your own and the only person you address as Sir, is myself. That title is reserved for those who have earned it.

A Valentine's Bind

When I sit, you will kneel at my feet. Understood?"

I nodded, still a little overwhelmed. He asked again a little louder this time. Enunciating each word.

"Do. You. Understand. Sub?"

"Yes Sir. I understand Sir."

I trembled remembering my spanking from earlier and the threat that a harsher punishment may ensue should I disobey.

He hummed a little as if not convinced of my understanding. Then gestured for me to walk in front of him as the doorman opened the door. Once more placing his hand in the small of my back and guided me forward.

CHAPTER SEVEN

Nicky

The noise, lights and music hit me like the
proverbial brick. *Stood to reason that the place would be
soundproofed considering it was a BDSM club.*

Still very conscious that I was wearing no panties
and walking a little oddly as a result. Trying to
remember to keep my eyes lowered was the hardest
part as there was so much to see. A myriad of sights
and sounds catching my attention.

A dazzling array of outfits caught my eye. Latex,
corsets, rubber, leather and every combination in
between. Male and female subs in a variety of dress
and undress. Skinny, fat, all sizes. Some had piercings
on display that I had never even heard of. Any
number of combinations of these. MF. MM, FF, and
also poly or poly-amorous where the number of
partners were multiplied in any number of
combinations.

Over in the distance was a a dungeon. I
recognised a St Andrews cross and a spanking bench

from the program I had watched, that had been the start of this whole journey. I would probably have continued to examine my surroundings but was brought back to earth by a couple of painful slaps to my bottom. Not gently ones, but a sharp reminder of what may happen. Dariel grabbed my hair and his hand was on my throat.

"Sub what were my instructions to you? You did acknowledge that you understood them little girl." He growled.

Focused now and God forbid gushing at his forceful manner.

What the hell?

"Sorry Sir. I will be a good girl now Sir. I've never seen anything like this before. There is so much to see and so much going on Sir." I explained.

He loosened his grip a little, but didn't let go.

"Good girl. As you are so new to this I will forgive you and there won't be a punishment this time. But. Be aware a second lapse and I will have no compunction not to do this here. In a very public manner. You will feel my hand on your arse. Your spanking earlier was just a taster. An OTK or over the knee sensual spanking. Be aware little girl. Punishment spankings are very different. You will carry my marks if you disobey me again. Understood sub?"

"Yes Sir. Sorry Sir." I answered contritely.

Well that put me firmly in my place. I thought as I lowered my eyes.

"Good girl. Come sub."

A Valentine's Bind

With that he led me over to some sofa's. Holding my arm, his other hand on my waist. As we approached I automatically went to sit down on the sofa and heard tutting in my ear.

"I thought you just agreed that you understood the rules, so recently given petal? Repeat them back to me. What were they again?" He ordered.

For a moment I just stood there trying to remember what rules he had relayed to me moments ago.

"Hmm let me think. You said to stay close to you Sir."

"Look at me now."

He took my face in his hands,holding it gently, but firmly as he looked deep into my eyes.

"My instructions were not to wander off. Address only myself as Sir. Kneel at my feet. Finally. Keep. Your. Eyes. Lowered." once again emphasising the last point.

"Oh."

"Oh? Not even Oh Sir? Petal it seems you have already forgotten the lesson I gave you this morning haven't you? I think this needs remedying immediately. I also have to inform you that in a D/s relationship a punishment is delivered and then the demeanour is forgotten and forgiven. We start with a clean slate once more. Much as you would scold a puppy for peeing on the rug. Stand now and put yourself over my lap sub."

His stern insistence demanded my obedience. Quaking with trepidation.

A Valentine's Bind

Surely this was just a test and he wouldn't spank me in public. Even as that thought hit me I felt warmth pool in my core and shuddered in anticipation. Feeling myself heat further. Yes I was embarrassed and a flush began down from my face to my chest. But the most horrifying fact to me was that I was turned on.

What is happening to me.

Dariel watched me closely. His eyes locked to mine. Studying me.

"Well...well... So you are a true exhibitionist. I would never have suspected as such until tonight."

The strangest thing was he looked proud of this fact.

He stood and pulled me close putting his hand up my skirt and quickly checked out just how turned on I was by fingering me. I jumped as for one it was unexpected and also some people were watching our discussion. I felt my pussy clench.

Oh shit! This was turning me on and humiliating me in equal parts. I worried.

"So wet petal. You are actually gushing and I felt you clench just then. Delicious."

Instead of removing his finger he then pushed two in, his hand on my bottom pulling me closer. Close enough that I could feel his raging hard on. I closed my eyes letting out a groan. I was so close to coming. Then I felt another smack on my bottom.

"Don't you dare cum. Resist. You cum when I give you permission little girl and not before or you will receive a much sterner punishment than I had planned." he ordered.

This focused my attention and I tried to think very unsexy thoughts to pull myself back. Dirty smelly socks and smelly feet. Anything to stop me cuming.

"Good girl."

With that he pulled me after him and over his lap. A sudden draft making me aware that my skirt had been lifted and my bare arse was on display for all to see. He held both my hands behind my back as before and said.

"I want to hear you count the spanks and thank me for each one. I am going to give you twenty spanks little one. If you disobey,wriggle or forget to thank me or count I will start over. Do you understand petal?"

"Yes Sir I understand." I gulped.

"Good girl. So now I will begin."

Only he didn't. He waited a few minutes I can only presume to heighten my anticipation and trepidation and damn him it worked. Impossibly I grew wetter still. Sodden at the thought of his spanking me and also that some people may be watching him spank me.

What was that all about?

Then when I least expected it he struck. Hard. The sound like a bull whip he spanked that hard. I grunted but after his warning managed to stay still and not struggle.

"One. Thank you Sir." I yelled.

He attacked first one cheek then the other for the

first five spanks in quick succession. I managed to deliver my thanks in a timely fashion between each. These spanks were far harder than those I received back at my flat. And tears slid down my cheeks unashamedly.

Then he changed his rhythm and the position of the spanks. Catching that sweet spot that hurts the most at the bottom most curve of my cheeks. I continued to count out. Sobbing loudly.

On occasion he would caress and check the skin but nothing like the sensual caresses of earlier. This was truly a punishment being delivered. The last spank administered and my thanks given. Despite the pain, tears and sobbing I could feel my juices running down my inner thigh.

I felt Sir place the kisses on my bottom then he began to stroke and sooth my raw throbbing rump. Murmuring in my ear.

"Such a good girl. My very good girl. Now you may cum petal."

With that he plunged three fingers deep inside me easily. His thumb working my now swollen and sensitive clit. My face heated followed by my body in quick succession as I exploded around his fingers. Throwing back my head I screamed out my climax as ecstasy overwhelmed me. His grip firm as he continued to play with me despite my squirming. My orgasms becoming painful as he whispered in my ear once more.

"I haven't finished with you yet sub. The next orgasm will be stronger and bigger than the last and you will take what I give you. Understand?"

"Yes. Thank you." I managed to croak out as I felt myself quicken.

I was no virgin but with all the guys I had had sex with it was "Wham, bam, thank you mam.".

Most came and went. If you know what I mean. Their own sexual gratification high on their "to do" list. My sexual gratification low on that list. This was extraordinary.

This time I swear I saw stars hit. Shuddering out my release once more. My heart trying to beat a way out of my chest in the process.

Once my climax began to ebb he slowly pulled out his fingers and I heard him suck on them. Such an erotic act, as I could hear him make small sounds of appreciation. As if he had just ate a delectable desert. He rearranged my dress and I detected a round of applause. I had completely forgotten where we were in those final moments of passion. Embarrassment once again hitting me. My face now the same hue as my arse.

He carefully righted me. Placing me on his lap. His expensive suit not hiding his significant hard on.

I had no problem looking down now as I was totally humiliated by my wayward behaviour in front of others.

He placed his finger gently under my chin lifted my gaze to his.

"Look at me sub. I want to see into those beautiful blue eyes and know what is going through that pretty little head of yours. That was beautiful

A Valentine's Bind

petal and you deserved that round of applause. I am so proud of you. You have excelled my expectations at every turn today. You were very brave. I can't wait to get inside your head and help you push through your barriers. I may even keep you. Who knows?"

With that he pulled me in to a devastatingly passionate kiss. His tongue tracing and teasing the edges of my mouth. Demanding that I open for him. I relinquished control and his tongue invaded my mouth. I wanted him inside me so badly. Pulling away he helped me stand on my shaky legs. Holding me until they settled.

CHAPTER EIGHT

Nicky

"Come. They have private rooms upstairs. This can't wait. I need to fuck you and I am sorely tempted to just bend you over and take you here and now. But, I think you would prefer s a little privacy my little sub."

"Yes Sir. I want you too. But, I think that would be a step too far despite our little show earlier." I sighed.

He guided me across the room, toward a flight of stairs in the far right hand corner close to the bar. He signalled the barman who seemed to know where he wanted to go and also set two bottles of water on the bar for him to pick up as he passed by. Sir grabbed them up and continued on at speed.

This gave me pause for thought and I stumbled a little.

Stupid girl. I thought. *This means nothing to him. It's just a fuck for him. One more willing victim. How many others has he taken up to these rooms? I am just*

A Valentine's Bind

another notch in his virtual headboard.

By the time we got to the first of the private rooms that was free, he may well had a hard on but, I was now dry as a bone. My lips set in a grim line. My body language closed. Screaming out my displeasure. He noticed it instantly. Despite this, he continued to guide me into the room, then left me standing as he closed the door.

Would he try and take me against my will? Would anyone even respond should I scream if he tried? Who knows? I felt very cold suddenly and began to tremble. *What had I got myself into? What was I even thinking to agree to all of this?*

Dariel approached me cautiously. As if I was a nervous filly and he was some kind of horse whisperer.

"Someone having second thoughts petal? Tell me what you are thinking. I am a Dominant, and not a mind reader by any means. I need you to articulate your concerns to me. So that we can address, them if possible."

His hard on now visibly diminished.

"Sit down and let's talk. You're shivering."

At this he led me over to one of the plush chairs. Grabbing a soft blanket off the bed. Wrapping it carefully around me as if I might break. Retrieving a bottle of water. Opened it and held it to my lips.

When did my lips and throat become so dry?

I sipped, relishing the cool refreshing water. Giving me much needed moisture.

"Now. I need to know what you are thinking

36

petal. Talk to me please."

My words came out in a rush. "How many women have you brought to these rooms? Am I just a piece of meat to you? A quick fuck then it's over?"

No Sir added this time. All thought of protocol and punishment gone from my mind. I needed answers to my questions. This had to stop now. This instant. My anger and agitation growing.

"Okay. Let's talk then" he said calmly. He sat on the bed facing me. A serious expression on his face.

"First of all. It doesn't matter exactly how many women I have brought here. That's subjective and bears no relation to what is happening here between us right now. The number is irrelevant, and meaningless. Right now, this is about the two of us. About us discovering more about each other. When I am in a Dom/sub relationship I am totally monogamous. This is not some quick fuck. This is me - your Dominant, taking control and demonstrating how I feel about you. I want to be able to understand, and please you. By far the biggest part of my power comes from giving you pleasure. A few minutes ago that was how you felt too. There is no denying it. Your pupils were dilated. Your pupils were so dilated very little blue was evident. You wanted this. Wanted me. I won't force you. That isn't what this is about. Safe. Sane. And consensual are the tenets of a good D/s. We. Petal. Are in a relationship now. If you want to walk away I suggest you do it now. I can drive you home this minute and you will never see me again. Is that truly what you want? But. If if like me, you want

A Valentine's Bind

to continue in this I will always try and give you what you need. Although sometimes it may not seem to be what you want. Make no mistake about this. I will nurture, protect and push you only if that is what you desire. A D/s relationship is not a one sided relationship."

He sat there patiently waiting, as what he said began to sink in, and I tried to understand what had happened.

The thing was. I did want this relationship, however crazy it may seem right now. I was also falling for my Dom. Hook, line and sinker.... That was never something I never expected to happen. Do I continue even though my feelings may never be reciprocated? Hell yeah. Whatever it was I wanted more of it. I have never felt more alive than over this last day or so. Dariel, (or Sir as I was beginning once again to think of him), had helped me experience more depth of feeling and emotion. Both physical and emotional than I ever imagined.

My decision made I looked straight into Sir's eyes telling him.

"Yes Sir. Forgive me. I need to learn to trust you and that may take some time. But, I am willing to try Sir, if you will still have me." I whispered.

He opened his arms wide and I rushed over. He enveloped me in his strong arms. Holding me close. Breathing me in and nuzzling my neck gently.

" I'm so sorry petal. I was rushing you. My fault. I should have explained everything to you simply and taken time to train you first. Taken things much slower. Doms can get it wrong sometimes too." He

A Valentine's Bind

said with a small laugh."We aren't infallible. You are far from a quick fuck and you happen to be the most beautiful piece of meat I have ever seen. Now. I think we need to head out of here but I am aware you aren't in University tomorrow. Are you working at the pub in the evening? Tonight I would you to like to make a stop at your flat. Pick up some of your belongings and you will come back to my place for the evening. Agreed?"

"Your place Sir? Absolutely Sir."

With that we kissed ferociously. He pulled away a little and bid me stand. His hand in mine as we began to head back down the stairs we had so recently ascended.

"If we carry on I will fuck you here. I would much rather take you to my place and fuck you there my pretty sub."

The barman looked astonished when we quickly returned through the bar. We exited the building at speed. Sir bidding goodbyes to anyone who tried to stop him, wanting to avoid conversation.

CHAPTER NINE

Nicky

Our journey back to my flat was quiet and contemplative. Although I caught him checking me out a few times.

Sir accompanied me to the flat where I threw some items of clothing and cosmetics into a small suitcase, which he insisted on carrying back to the car for me. Double checking the flat was safely locked up and all the appliances turned off.

I wondered *Are all Doms more than a little OCD about these things?*

I didn't have a clue where his "home" was. So I was eager to see what it may be.

Maybe an expensive flat in town or a rural retreat? Who knew?

He headed out of Manchester and and were following signs to Cheshire. Soon we were heading towards Lymm. In my eyes a pretty posh place to live.

Finally, the car slowed down on a small country lane and then turned down a private road. Lights

A Valentine's Bind

shining off a little way in the distance. So, maybe not a flat but a house of some kind. After about five minutes we drew up in front of a gorgeous modern house. Lots of glass and clean lines. High tech looking. The outside security lights were on and at the press of a button on Sir's keyring, lights popped on inside the house.

"Wow. This is beautiful. I love it Sir."

"I had it built a few years ago to my exact specifications. I can control the lights and heating through an app and the device on my keyring as you saw. It has solar panels and is as green as I could have it built. Save the planet and all that." He quipped.

"The doors are especially reinforced. I didn't want to come back from a business trip to an empty house. The alarm system is state of the art. Come on in. You are shivering. I hope you remembered to bring a coat or warm jacket with you?"

We entered a large open hallway with stairs running up the centre and a galleried landing visible that wrapped around at the top.

"I will put some coffee on then take you upstairs and show you around. The grand tour, as it were. There is one room in particular I would like to show you. We will spend quite some time in there."

I raised my eyebrows at this remark,wondering whether it may be a room like the one in *Fifty Shades of Grey*. The red room of pain. As we climbed the stairs I looked around in wonder.

The artwork alone, if it was genuine., must be worth a fortune. In fact everywhere I looked I saw that he had

A Valentine's Bind

expensive tastes. *What on earth did he do for a living?*

This left me with more questions than answers.

What did I know about him. Very little yet, he knew reams about me.

He led me around the upper floor starting on the right hand side where the guest bedrooms were. All decorated quite differently. The first one in shades of purple and Lavender. One in shades of browns and beige. The final bedroom all white with cushions and detailing picked out in red. There were two family sized bathrooms between the three room. Both of these had pristine white suites in, with all the usual mod cons, including a large tub in each. No expense spared. But, so far no red room of pain As far as I could see we had been in all of the rooms except the main bedroom.

Sir picked up my suitcase which he had left at the top of the stairs, then led me toward the left and what I supposed would be the Master bedroom. He placed my suitcase at the end of the bed, and I spent a few minutes looking around. The room was decorated in shades of black, white and grey. Very masculine. No throw pillows in here and very minimalist décor. Sleek black furniture finished the look.

"Now the piece de resistance." Sir announced with a little flourish." My absolute favourite room in the whole house."

As he led me towards a pair of doors set to the left hand side. Nodding at one immediately to the left of it, he indicated. "That is my en-suite. You can investigate in there later petal. This on the other hand is my dungeon."

And there it was in all it's glory. His very own red room of pain.

He went to explain. "The whole room is soundproofed and can act as a safe room in an emergency. I have CCTV all over the house and can view the screens either in here, or my study. The alarm company have also got access, but the dungeon, and my master suite of rooms I am able to restrict when necessary. Although, after seeing how much you enjoyed public play this evening I could make an exception on occasion."

I felt the colour rise in my cheeks at that remark, and cleared my throat.

"Maybe not just yet then Maybe a boundary to work up to over time. " His eyes sparkled, smile broad once again revealing those dimples. "We have an array of equipment at our disposal. The obligatory St Andrew's cross and a spanking bench. A Queening chair..."

Seeing my curious expression he proceeded.

"I will explain this one to you later. With a demonstration possibly. Of course a super king sized bed with a difference. This one has straps and rings set into it and a very nice set of stocks too. Rings and hoists set into the ceiling. Of course the contents of the drawers may interest you also."

As he pulled out each drawer in order for me to purvey the contents. Some items I recognised others I could only get at their uses. Floggers, canes, crops, paddles and other implements I didn't know the

A Valentine's Bind

names of were set neatly out on the walls. The place was littered with every object you could think of. Toys of all description, including coils of rope in different shades. At each new discovery I felt myself gush a little more. His hard on now difficult to ignore. Especially as I had spotted him adjusting his accoutrements a few times during this latter part of my tour.

As I leaned over to take a closer look at the spanking bench, he took advantage. Pushing me further over and as quick as a flash had me fastened with my legs spread and my skirt raised.

"Hmmm is there any more delicious a sight than this? I think not. You have an absolute peach of an arse. Have I told you this?"

He reached between my legs. His fingers finding my wet folds and with a devilish laugh announced.

"Now I am going to fuck you princess that loves to be treated like a slut. My good girl. My petal."

I heard his zipper then heard some shuffling and noises as he undressed. The plush carpet meaning he could go barefoot comfortably.He padded around approaching from the front. His magnificent hard on jutting near to my lips. I licked my lips salaciously, wanting a taste of the precum I could see. Tantalising as it glistened. Almost as if Sir could read my mind he asked.

"Would you like a taste petal?"

As he moved closer. I swiped my tongue across the crown, swirling it around and back across the tip. Swallowing down his salty musky precum in the

A Valentine's Bind

process. He thrust his cock between my open eager lips and I had no choice but to take him in. Choking and gagging in the process. Then he would pull out allowing me to take a quick breath. Drool dripped down my chin. Stepping back he tutted a little.

"Greedy girl. Plenty of time for you to worship my cock later. I have plans for that sweet mouth. If fact I have detailed plans for all of your holes. Although technically they are all mine in any case. To do with what I will. Now to finish what was started at the club."

Disappearing from view I then felt his cock nudging at my entrance as he took himself balls deep in one almighty thrust.

Sweet Jesus. Full to the brim.

I wiggled as best I could. Wanting more but he held still, and ordered.

"What is you want petal? You have to spell it out for me sweetie. Beg me, and you may get what you need. If I don't feel you have begged me sufficiently I may withhold my cock and my cum."

"Please fuck me Sir." I begged in frustration.

"Louder sub. I can't hear you. What did you say?"

I screamed out in desperation.

"Please fuck me Sir. I need you inside me. I need you to fill me up with your cum."

He began to piston in and out. Almost pulling out, leaving just the very tip inside. Tormenting me. I tried to push back despite my restraints. His hand reached to hold my throat as he ordered.

A Valentine's Bind

"Don't you dare cum until I tell you to little girl. You WILL wait for permission."

One hand now squeezing my nipples hard and the other moved to my labia. Pushing through my folds and circling my swollen sensitive clit. Once again tormenting me. Pushing me hard.

"Please Sir I need to cum now. Please let me cum." I sobbed.

He let me wait and beg a little more then stretched forward to whisper in my ear. "Cum for me. I want to hear you scream."

And I did.

Feeling his hot sperm hit my cervix I started to clench around his cock. Milking him.

A random thought hit me that once again we had used no protection. Then that thought, fleeting was gone as quickly as it came. Mindless bliss replacing any meaningful thought processes I was having. As stars appeared behind my eyes. Heat travelling through my body like quick-fire. As he continued pumping in to me until he too was spent.

Both covered in a sheen of perspiration. Quickly released from my restraints, as he checked my circulation. Rubbing the skin gently taking time to check the integrity of the skin. He picked me up and carried my boneless body through to the bedroom. The covers already pulled back in anticipation. Laying me down with care he climbed in and snuggled close. My head once again on his chest, listening to his racing heart. The solid feel of his chest with the aroma I now knew so well. Of musk, perspiration, aftershave and his own unique woodsy smell permeated the air. One hand stroking my hair as the other traced slow leisurely circles on my back. My eyes drifted closed and I slept like a newborn.

CHAPTER TEN

Dariel

I awoke refreshed and well rested. As I usually suffered to a degree from insomnia, this was a welcome change.

Settling on my elbow I watched Nicky, my petal, sleep. Her hair spread across the pillow in a silken fan. Soft noises and on occasion gentle snores the only sounds. But,it didn't detract from her beauty. Porcelain skin. A smattering of freckles across her nose and cheeks. My little one. The pull I felt toward this little sub far greater than I had ever felt before, and I was trying to quantify it.

A Dom/sub relationship generally was more involved, and deep than that of a vanilla or 'nilla relationship. Possibly due to the openness and need for truthfulness and communication. Trust vital.

What made this time so different? The connection was alive. The zing of electricity that shoots through me when I touch her. Or her me. The surge I feel as she bows to my will and obeys me, tangible.

A Valentine's Bind

My need to now keep and collar her, overwhelming. Reaching over I stroke her cheek tenderly. Even in her sleep she leans into my touch.

No. What am I thinking. I have to help her that is all she asked of me. Then, find her a suitable Dom.

I decided to distract myself so showered in one of the guest bedrooms so as not to disturb my sleeping angel. Then went downstairs to prepare breakfast.

CHAPTER ELEVEN

Nicky

The next morning I awoke to find myself in bed once again, alone. A glass of fresh orange on the side table with a single red rose lying next to it. Smiling I stretched, leaned over, picked up the glass and slowly drank it down. My fingers trailing over the rose.

Just like my Dom, beautiful and soft but also wearing thorns.

Who knew that pleasure and pain could excite the senses so?

I opened the door to the en-suite, and after some trial and error worked out how to use the shower. I smelled of sex and sweat. The sexy smell I liked, the sweat not so much. I ached all over and the shower eased this, refreshing me. My body and pussy tender to touch.

I dried myself and took a look in the mirror at the marks Sir had left. The red bloom had gone but in it's wake there were the first blossoming bruises there. Evidence of my submission. Parts of my bottom now

A Valentine's Bind

were becoming black and blue. Badges of honour in the kink world. I actually expected there to be more bruising and examined them closely. They hurt a little when I pressed but nothing I couldn't stand. I also had fingertip bruises on my hips from when we had sex in the shower that first time.

I spotted a couple of white fluffy dressing gowns on the back of the bathroom door and pulled one on.

Retrieving my glass from the bedroom I went off to check out the downstairs and hopefully locate Sir. Once out of the bedroom, as I descended, the smell of cooking bacon pulled me in the right direction. I thought about my tour last night and how it was to include the downstairs rooms. That was, until we got to the red room of pain and the tour ended abruptly. *Only it wasn't a red room of pain as it was tan, black, white and no red to be seen. The brown room of pain just sounded wrong. No. I needed a name that was just mine.* Something to ponder later.

I found the kitchen and Sir quite quickly. The kitchen was just as wonderful as the rest of the house and equally modern. A chef's dream. Black kitchen units, shiny black granite worktops and stainless steel in abundance including the huge range. Sir had on low slung pyjama pants and a tight white t-shirt, that outlined his amazing body. No slippers. Then I realised it didn't matter about the slippers as there was underfloor heating that I could feel as I also was barefoot.

"Good morning petal. I hope you like full English? I have set up the breakfast bar for us. Help

A Valentine's Bind

yourself to juice. It is set in a jug there. Coffee is on
the hotplate keeping warm. Won't be long."

The breakfast bar was an immense granite unit in
the kitchen set near to the a set of glass doors that
stretched across the entire back wall of the kitchen.
The views of the Cheshire countryside outside made
prettier by the frost. I poured more orange and
wandered closer to see.

He came up behind me, putting his arms around
my waist, pulled me close.

"Beautiful isn't it? This is why I chose this
particular spot. I own as far as you can see. Didn't
want anyone building houses or putting any building
in my line of sight. Come. Breakfast is ready now.
Toast?"

I stood there a moment longer.

*How much was Sir worth that he could even do that?
Land isn't cheap especially in this part of Cheshire.*

I sat down and examined my breakfast. Wincing
a little as I felt the bruises on my bottom sting a tiny
bit as I sat on the hard bar stool. Looked back down at
my plate and thought.

All my favourite things Yum. And began to tuck
in. *Sir seemed to be on a mission to control what I ate,
drank, wore. When or whether I was allowed to cum.
Control freak much?* I thought to myself smiling.

"Something amuse you sub? Care to share that
thought?" He enquired.

"Just wondering if all Doms have a form of
OCD and a compulsion to control everything Sir?
That's all."

A Valentine's Bind

He took a bite of food, chewing, thinking this through.

" Maybe so petal. I hadn't thought of it quite like that but you may have a valid point."

We chatted through breakfast and I realised this could be an opportunity to discover more about Sir.

"Sir. Can I ask you some questions? You know so much about me but I know very little about you?"

"Fire away petal." He responded.

I turned to face him as we were side by side.

"What sort of work do you do Sir? This place must have cost a pretty penny. Saville Row suits, fancy car..."

"Cars."

"Sorry?" I replied.

"Cars plural. Sir. That is my day to day work car I have a few others in the garage out back. I can show you them later if you like?" He stated.

"Cars then." I reiterated.

Cars plural I thought. *And. That was his run around! Goodness know what the others were.*

"So. Work?" I began then added "Sir"

"Sorry. I didn't realise I hadn't told you. I own an electronics firm. My company actually makes and manufactures all these fancy gadgets and alarms I am so fond of. I have companies across the UK and abroad. Including some located in America and Canada."

"I only know your first name Sir. You do have a last name I presume?" I joked.

"Of course. Dariel Pearson. My firm is Pearson

53

A Valentine's Bind

Electronics. If you want to google me later on, feel free petal." he teased me back. "My life as a Dom is private and although I don't use a contract for my D/s relationships I will have to ask you to sign a non-disclosure document. No big deal as you can imaging the publicity would hurt my business should details of my predilections be exposed in public."

I laughed a little myself at this, and explained.

"I am so glad you won't want me to sign a contract. That was the thing I hated the most in the book and film *Fifty Shades of Grey*. Bored me to death the way it was repeated so many times. I see no problem in signing the non-disclosure document though Sir."

"Yes. *Fifty Shades* caused some consternation within the BDSM Community. But, I digress. Anything else you need to know petal?" he countered.

Then it struck me. A vital piece of information I needed to know for my own peace of min.

"Why aren't we using condoms when we have sex? Sir." I enquired.

He paused watching me closely. Then responded.

"Because. When I asked you about using protection that very first night you said, and I quote."I got this covered. Don't sweat it." So, I surmised either you were on the pill or had an implant of some kind petal."

I suddenly felt sick to my stomach. Drunk me must have been so desperate to get laid, that I had lied through my back teeth and risked getting pregnant or an STD. I sat in stunned silence not sure what to say or do next.

Morning after pill? I thought

"I gather by the fact you have become dumbstruck, and are also now ashen in colour that this was a lie. If so I think we have already missed the opportunity of the "morning after" pill. Unless I am mistaken." He stated as he typed into his phone.

Practical as well as Dominant and a bit of a mind reader as well.

"Lucky you." He chirped "According to my search it works three to five days after sex. So, I presume one of our errands today will be to procure some for you. While we are at it I suggest we arrange for adequate protection for the future. I have no shortage of condoms at my disposal already. Rest assured. I prefer not to use them if possible though."

He made is sound so simple. I felt a little better learning that there was a pretty simple solutions.

Thank goodness for small mercies.

"As soon as we have finished breakfast I suggest we make that a priority. My list of fetishes does not include "Breeders" luckily for you or I may have denied you access to the means to prevent pregnancy." He added.

With that astonishing remark we concluded breakfast, tidied the kitchen and made our way back upstairs.

Who even knew that such a fetish existed. I didn't for one.

Sir must have hung my clothes, as I slept this

A Valentine's Bind

morning as when I went in search of my suitcase he directed me to a wardrobe in the far corner. As I made my way across I got "the look" as I now thought of it.

"What do you think you are doing little girl. I thought you understood the few basic rules we have in place so far? I get to choose what you wear each day. Not you. I think seeing as how you will be visiting both a chemist and a doctor today I will go for something fairly conservative. Underwear of course."

He looked through the items I had brought with me choosing a plain white bra and panties, jeans, jumper, socks and trainers.

"There you go. You dress while I gather my clothes and dress. Understood?" he asked.

"Yes Sir" I chanted back happily.

It was actually easier when I didn't have to make all my decisions.

He started to hum a tune as he disappeared into a larger walk in closet on the opposite side of the room. This was strangely comforting. Dressing casually in a pair of expensive black jeans, snug blue jumper, black leather lace up boots completing the ensemble.

Did he know how absolutely gorgeous he even looked? Probably not. I mused.

I grabbed up my jacket and he appeared wearing a leather jacket. Every item he wore screamed money. Including his watches. He decided once again to use his "run around" as he wanted to get me organised with both the pill and the pill today.

First we visited a large supermarket that had a

chemist attached. We had to see the chemist as they don't just hand this stuff over willy nilly. Sir insisted on being present which was pretty unnerving as the chemist proceeded to ask when my last period was etc. etc. In fact he answered questions on my behalf a few times. He insisted on paying for the prescription, despite me whipping out my purse and trying to pay for myself.

After all I thought *It was my own stupid fault that I was in this fix in the first place.*

No he was in command and my Dom and had this covered. From there he escorted me to a local clinic. Well it stood to reason he would be well versed in all these.

I can't be the first he has had to accompany like this? I studied him as he drove. *So in command. Even in the car. In everything he did. So controlling.*

Despite my reservations, his taking command felt right somehow. Not just in the bedroom where I melted when he praised me. But, in everything else he did.

Snap out of it Nicky. He will tire of you soon enough then replace you with another

It was almost as if I had a devil on one shoulder and angel on the other.

CHAPTER TWELVE

Nicky

Once everything was sorted to his satisfaction we returned to my flat and I made us some hot drinks. Taking note of the distinct lack of goodies in my cupboard and fridge. I now had a supply of the pill, plus a huge box of condoms. I couldn't bring myself to say nowe didn't need them and that we probably had boxes of the things already. I had also just taken the morning after pill. All in all a very unglamourous morning, but at least I wouldn't be pregnant. My flat looked very inauspicious compared to the luxury of Sir's elegant home. But beggars can't be choosers can they, my mum always said.

"Tomorrow we will visit my solicitors and sign the non-disclosure documents if you are still agreeable. I have a few things I want to teach you today petal. First of all there are some positions I will expect you to practice until you have them perfected."

He showed me some pictures on his phone. Of a naked girl, collared where she was kneeling, kneeling

A Valentine's Bind

but her ass in the air, stood and lay on the floor. On all the pictures her legs were wide open.

Bit of a theme going on here. That doesn't look too difficult. I thought.

I hadn't spoken yet. Just observed.

"Not saying very much? Are we petal. Let me explain a little more. These positions allow me to inspect you, and also make you available to me should I desire to touch you. Does that make better sense. Now strip naked and this can be our first lesson."

With that he stood. I sat there a little while longer then I decided .

Why not try? It's not like he hasn't seen me naked before. Yet, each time I still felt a little bit shy and inadequate. Like any other female I knew I had numerous failings. I pondered.

I started to undress tossing my clothes over the back of the sofa until I heard the tutting noise.

I stopped and looked at him asking. "What's the problem?"

He tutted louder still moved closed and swatted my bottom hard, twice.

"Ow! What was that for?" I demanded.

"First of all you will learn to fold your clothes like a good little girl. Secondly I failed to hear you say Sir once again."

I blushed. *Epic fail Nicky. Oops*

"Sorry Sir. I will try and remember Sir"

"There is no try. Only do." He quipped back.

Wasn't that a line from Star Wars? Yoda if I remember rightly.

A Valentine's Bind

I picked up and folded my discarded clothes and then continued to strip. Feeling more than a little exposed. Standing there starkers in my living room in broad daylight.

How bizarre.

"Stop right now little one. Your reticence is broadcasting loud and clear. You have a beautiful body and should be proud of it. If I tell you you are beautiful then merely accept it as the truth. It is usual for a you to thank your Dom. To me you are exquisite. Okay?"

"Yes Sir. Thank you Sir." I acknowledged.

"First position where you are kneeling back on your heels. Legs apart. Hands palm up on your thighs please petal."

And so we went through each position in turn. Sir adjusting my stance. More often than not that included my having to open my legs farther. Until finally he was happy with me.

"Now gather some more of your clothing as the next part will involve access to my dungeon. I am very pleased with you my good girl."

He watched with interest as I gathered a few more of my meagre possessions and added.

" We will call and pick up a few items for you on the way back to mine."

With that remark he left me to pack and I could hear him talking to someone on the phone. I didn't have much to pack as being a student my budget didn't stretch to fancy clothes. Or even basic clothing. I had that one decent outfit for when we partied and

A Valentine's Bind

painted the town red.

True to his word we stopped a a large shopping centre and called in a few shops. Gathering bags already packed with clothing. I tried to peak into one and it was quickly taken off me and placed in the boot of the car. Reprimanded for even trying.

God knew what he had bought me.

Once back at his I was yet again told to strip, and take my positions. Satisfied once more that I truly understood what he wanted I was instructed to stay in the kneeling position he refereed to as waiting, and listen.

"From today when we are here you will remain naked at all times unless I put out clothes for you to wear. Understand petal?"

I nodded.

He waited.

"Yes Sir." I acknowledged.

"Good girl. You will learn to mark my words this way. Even when I am not here, you will observe this. Remember I have camera's everywhere and can see if you disobey. I will notify you by some means, either email, text or phone call to alert you to my imminent arrival. I expect you to be knelt in the hall in the waiting position for my return. Understood?"

"Yes Sir."

"Come. The only other item you will wear is what we call a collar of consideration. I expect you to read the books I will leave for you. These will give you an insight into the Lifestyle and you are to write down any questions you have so that we may discuss

A Valentine's Bind

them each day. This will help you understand your submission and some of the many fetishes."

I had followed him upstairs during this discussion and we were now once again in the dungeon.

"Kneel." He ordered. And I did.

He rummaged through a few of the drawers and came back with what looked like a large dog collar and some other items that turned out to be wrist and ankle restraints. He placed the collar around my neck and I was surprised how comfortable it was. It was red leather with a soft wick lining. A ring evident at the front that reminded me of the one that the slave wore to the club. I looked to see if he had a leash. As if he read my mind he explained.

"No leash. Not here in the house at any rate."

He indicated and I gave him my wrists in turn as he placed the restraints there. Next were the ones for my ankles and he checked to be sure they didn't chafe. The he bid me rise. He studied me closely and smiled.

"Beautiful. You suit red. I didn't expect that with your auburn hair."

He pushed a errant strand of hair behind my ear and stroked my cheek gently.

Training continued throughout the day and I was introduced in turn to some of the items in the drawers. Each passed to me in turn for inspection and he answered any and all my questions.

There were floggers, ropes, tawse, paddles, bullet vibrators, crops, whips,nipple clamps. The list went on until I was almost dizzy, yet extremely moist. Sir's deep evening voice explaining intimate detail

A Valentine's Bind

how he intended to use each and every item. Telling
me I would grow to need, love, want and beg for him
pleasure and pain involved.

He demonstrated a number of items. Tying me
to the cross and spanking bench in turn. The most
embarrassing was his use of what he termed a "small"
butt plug. My eyes must have looked like saucers and
I gulped as he fastened me down. The butt plugs
would be increased in size. He explained. Until my
ass was "trained", He then went on in minute detail
how he would then fuck my virgin hole.

Lube was trickled on my bottom and then I felt
Sir rub gently around my rosebud. It felt strange and
dirty but as he continued to probe , then finally push a
digit into my bottom. Bidding me to push back and
relax to allow him in. I felt myself quicken. He
continued to stimulate me, rimming my anus and I
could feel him then use two fingers opening me wider.
Next something cold and hard was pressed there, and
with a little push it was fully seated. My sodden core
letting him know that this was a turn on. He slid the
plug in and out a few times and finally whispered.

"Cum for me."

My orgasm hit me out of the blue.
Overwhelming me as I spasm around the fingers that
he inserted fingers easily into my pussy as he said
those words. If this felt full, what would his cock feel
like back there. He continued to fondle me until I was
limp and sated. Pulsing still. He kissed both my
cheeks and gently removed the plug. I heard him
drop it in the steel sink.

A Valentine's Bind

He untied me, pulled me on his lap on the bed as he cuddled and kissed me. Letting me know what a good girl I was, and how proud he was of me.

CHAPTER THIRTEEN

Dariel

Her response to everything I do was a delight. She effortlessly gives herself to me. Although the beguiling brattiness was still in evidence at times. I never liked easy or simple. I couldn't wait to push her limits and mark her as mine. So that others truly knew who she really belonged to.

She tantalised me.

One minute she is a firebrand. The next surrendering her very all to me. She never ceased to amaze me as she yielded to my every whim.I need to either learn to harden my heart, or make her mine but was holding myself back from making this important decision.

She consumed my every waking thought. The Dom in me wanting to both protect and sear my very soul into her flesh. Was I too ambitious.

CHAPTER FOURTEEN

Nicky

Our days passed quickly.

Each day he pushed and taught me and in the evenings when I wasn't working we discussed my queries over fetishes and submission. The sex beyond amazing. Excruciating yet at the same time magnificent. I shattered at his touch at a word now. Pain and pleasure taking me so high that I flew. I learned this had a name. Subspace. An out of body experience.

Time had flown so fast and it was now four weeks since our first day together and also Valentine's Day. Poetic really. My world had turned upside down since we had met.

What would I do when he tired of me? How could I ever find someone who knew me so well? Sure, there were plenty of Doms out there. He had even sat me down and showed me where they could be found both on the internet and attending events called a munch. I had learned that there were more or less a social gathering of like minded kinksters. Some time play would happen, sometimes not. Conversations at these event are pretty stimulating ranging from gardening to fisting! Very liberating. My only problem was remembering that I couldn't talk this openly with everyone.

I had returned to University and had classes through the day and Sir made sure my work was up to date. I joked he had become a daddy Dom when he did this and he didn't take that well. Resulting in a very sore bottom that I didn't forget in a hurry. My friends were constantly asking me out and wanted to know details of my new boyfriend. What could I tell them I hardly knew how to articulate it myself. The thing was that I was a more than willing participant. I came alive with my Sir in so many ways. It wasn't all the kink and sex either as we would talk about everything and nothing too. We had similar tastes in art, music, films, any number of things.

Tonight was a special night as not only was it Valentine's Day but it was four weeks to the day since he first took me to his club. This was also the first time I would get to wear my collar of consideration in public. It felt far longer than four weeks to me. My life before I met Sir paled into the background. What was my life before that pivotal night when I agreed in a drunken stupor to be his submissive.

Trying to throw off this morose mood I began to research for an assignment I had to complete the following week, but not with much success as I was too distracted. Putting on some of my favourite music to play in the background. *Hey Now* by *London*

A Valentine's Bind

Grammar.

Drew myself a nice deep bubble bath and then I would shave. I shaved everyday now. For both mine and Sir's pleasure. He insisted on shaving me the very first time which was scary and erotic at the same time. I buffed my nails and had just finished painting them when I heard the key in the lock.

Bugger I would smudge my nails when I kneel for Sir and have to start all over again. I grumbled to myself.

We each had a key now but woe betide I left the flat messy or bought the wrong type of food as he checked it out on a regular basis and I was duly rewarded or punished accordingly. Although to be honest both were an incentive I mused

My heart rate increased, like an incessant drum. He had this effect on me every time he came near. His texts and phone calls causing the same effect.

"Good evening my beautiful little girl." He greeted me.

I wasted no time reaching him and kneeling on impulse. Wet nails forgotten. Displaying myself brazenly for him. What was so hard to do in the first place, now second nature. I was his, and his only. With all my flaws and imperfections he was always ramrod hard at the sight and smell of me.

This is the power I feel as his submissive. The depths of my feelings constant and all unremitting. I marvelled.

I looked up into his eyes. Those oh so beautiful steel blue eyes. Tears began to pool in mine at the thought of losing him . Of losing this. The very real possibility too hard to bare. This could only be short

A Valentine's Bind

lived as he had only agreed to train me to help me. Once he thought my training was over I would be set free. My collar removed and eventually given to another.

"Petal? Is everything alright? Why the tears? Tonight is a celebration and our first visit to the club as Dom/sub. Wipe your eyes silly. I have some presents for you. Something special for you to wear tonight. Come."

With that he reached out and took my hand in his, pulling me into his firm embrace. My head nestled against his shoulder inhaling his distinctive musky smell interwoven with his woodsy aftershave. I felt safe and protected. Taking my hand he pulled me along , much like an eager schoolboy. Sir was in a really good mood today. His dimples as he smiled bringing me out of my funk. He placed the bags on the bed and tipped each out, unveiling the contents. A stunning corset in black lace, trimmed with red satin roses and zwaroski crystals. A matching pair of black satin shoes, lace topped black stockings and a teeny tiny matching thong. The heels about four inches high, I was still learning how to walk in higher heels.

The corset was a work of art, but that wasn't what caught my eye. It was a demi-cup therefore my nipples would be openly on display.

I could feel his eyes on me, waiting for my reaction. Perhaps this was a test of sorts. I knew my reaction would set the mood for the evening. Looking up I sought his eyes.

"Exquisite Sir. Thank you Sir." I gushed and he

A Valentine's Bind

let out an audible sigh and visibly relaxed.

He was already dressed in an immaculate black suit, crisp white shirt with cuff-links gleaming. Black leather boots and a scarlet red tie. Perhaps the tie was an attempt to coordinate with my outfit. He tipped out another larger bag and inside was an expensive looking dress-coat made of a delicious satin fabric. It was a brilliant scarlet red colour.

Now it was my turn to heave a sigh of relief. I was going to have something suitable over my corset for our dinner date. He smiled, his dimples showing once more. He knew me too well it seems.

"Dress quickly little girl. We eat out first of all. Where we ate the first time. I presume you will be wanting to keep the coat on in there." He chuckled.

I stroked the satin, feeling how soft it was. Perfect. Not too heavy so that I would get too warm in the restaurant.

Clever Sir. I thought.

Eager now to please him I began to dress. But sexily. Like a striptease in reverse as I lingered over putting on my stockings. Once dressed in my ensemble I walked over to the mirror to examine my reflection.

How hot did I look? Erotic too.

The corset fitted me like a glove and my boobs were supported. Nipples extended. Especially after Sir gave them a little help by tweaking them. Sir assisted me with my coat-dress. Once wrapped around and tied I looked fairly respectable. That is if you discounted the fact that my nipples poked through the slinky fabric of the dress-coat.

I did a little twirl and curtsied for Sir. His rapt expression letting me he approved. He then escorted me outside and instead of one of his cars, a huge sleek black limo sat waiting at the kerb. Tonight it seemed, I was to be Cinderella.

A chauffeur appeared and opened the door for us greeting us making sure we were comfortable as we set off in style. Excited, as I had never been in a limo before. Sir amused by my very obvious pleasure, pulled me closer and onto his lap.

"New experience petal?" He enquired.

"Yes Sir." I answered eagerly.

"Just so you know. This will be the first of many firsts for you tonight."

I clenched at that thought. He loved to put me on my back foot. I had learned that he used anticipation as a big part of my training. Like Pavlov's dogs, but instead of salivating, somewhere else became sodden instead.

We pulled up to *The Ivy* and once again we remained still as the chauffeur appeared to open the door . Sir slipped out first proffering his hand. A gentleman first and foremost despite having a wicked sadistic nature. Once inside the restaurant we were greeted enthusiastically by the *Maître D*, seated efficiently at the same booth we occupied last time.

Menu's appeared and of course Sir took both.

Sparking water, ice and lemon and olives for starters. Instead of steak this time Sir decided on the salmon, salad and new potatoes. Strawberries dipped in chocolate for desert. Delicious but not too heavy.

I kept my knees apart waiting for Sir to use his clever skillful fingers but was actually a little disappointed when he didn't. My anticipation continuing to build. Once we had finished eating I asked to be excused to the toilets. My nervousness having an unwanted affect on my bladder.

As I rose Sir beckoned me over and whispered in my ear.

"Be sure not to play petal. I will know if you have and you understand there will be dire consequences should you disobey me?"

"Yes Sir. I mean no Sir." I won't play." I stammered.

To be honest until he said this I hadn't even thought about it. Now I could think of nothing else and my fingers were itching to play. In the Lifestyle they call this a mind-fuck. Doms love to mess with and control their sub's psyche. My anticipation rose another notch. The little new thong was saturated with my juices. I will have to hitch up coat-dress when I sit in the limo or there will be a incriminating damp patch for all to see.

As I returned, he rose at my approach, and once again his palm was placed in the small of my back as he guided me out. Bidding good night as he did.

How could someone with such meticulous manners have such an evil sadistic streak? And why on earth did I love him all the more for it?

I stopped suddenly. Nearly stumbling as Sir continued to push me along.

A Valentine's Bind

I realised what I had just thought. *Love? When did my lust and affection turn to love?*

I still hadn't moved.

I looked up into his eyes and it hit.

I did love him. God help me I did, and there was nothing I could do about it . When he decided to end our contract I knew it would cause my heart to splinter, not just break.

CHAPTER FIFTEEN

Dariel

The night was going so well. Beautifully. Completely according to plan. My mind games were beginning to take effect. No need to feel her to know how much they had affected her. I could smell her beguiling scent of her honey quite distinctly.

Then suddenly she has disconnected and looks sad.

The flush she had on her cheeks and neck has paled.

Eyes not as dilated.

Something has gone badly amiss. But what?

CHAPTER SIXTEEN

Nicky

*I had to make it through this evening. I would do this
for my Sir.* I decided.

Once in the car we both sat quietly. Sir had
obviously picked up on my suddenly sombre mood
and I didn't know how to mend it. I looked out of the
window aimlessly, unseeing and despondent.

Lucky for me Sir took matters into his own hands.
Grabbing my hair forcefully he pulled me closed.
Plundered my mouth with sensuous strokes of his
tongue playing on my closed lips. Licking and tracing
the seam until I opened up to him. Allowing him
entrance as he continued to probe. He tasted of
strawberries... chocolate... and sex.

I let out a breathy moan. The atmosphere no
longer sombre but intense as he drew me to him. My
heart beat escalating. The blood rushing in my ears.
He leaned back to look in my eyes. Letting out a
ragged breath as he traced a path along my jaw, down
to my collarbone. Frissons of heat scoring a path

75

A Valentine's Bind

across my skin.

"Better?"

"Yes Sir. Much better." I whispered.

The limo pulled directly in front of the entrance to the club and the door was opened. It seemed only moments since we had left the restaurant but it must have been at least twenty minutes. Sir, as usual, alighted first. Then reached for my hand. But this time as I stepped out and began to move forward he stood in my path.

Slowly and languorously he undid the belt on my coat-dress, parting it with a flourish pulling my coat from my shoulders. Then he passed my coat to the chauffeur. The cool evening air have an immediate effect. My nipples hard and elongated as Sir and the chauffeur openly admired them. The chauffeur even licked his lips.

"Perfect" Sir said "Ready for my next surprise?"

He withdrew a small black velvet pouch from his pocket, tipping the contents into the palm of his hand.

Picking up the first object in his nimble fingers he pulled and flicked at my right nipple. Extending it further then applied a small silver nipple clamp with tiny red bells dangling from it. He looked me in the eye as he tightened it, as I let out a gasp. Happy with the effect he applied the second one.

He then pulled out of his pocket my usual red collar and placed that about my neck. I felt proud to wear his collar and he led me into the club. Sir had said that now I was wearing my collar I could take some time to look around safely. My collar would tell others that I am taken, so not to touch or approach me without permission.

The Master and his slave we had seen on our previous visit, were already seated inside. He sat on one of the sofa's, and his slave happily knelt at his feet. Adoring eyes on her Master. I felt a pang of jealousy, they looked so happy.

Sir sat alongside and I took my place at his feet as I had been taught. Feeling a little exposed, but as the slave was once again almost naked felt a bit better. I looked around, as best I could from this position. Taking in all the sights and sounds once more. There was so much to see. Then I realised that Sir was talking to me, and looked up contrite.

"Petal. Ahh ... there you are. Distracted again I see. I have to admit it can be a tad daunting when you are new. It is a long time since I first set foot in a club like this. Let me introduce you petal. This is my very good friend Simon. He is SirFucksToy on Fetlife. So sometimes goes by that name too. This is his beautiful wife, and slave Lily. Lily goes by the name of SirsToy on Fetlife."

I wasn't too sure how you went about this, but acknowledged and said hello. Remembering that I called him by name and not Sir, as instructed.

Lily and I were permitted to sit closer.Just in front and given permission to talk. We quickly realised that we were both the same age and Lily was in University and a student Doctor. She was studying at Manchester University. Lily talked about all the different events they attended and said she would ask

A Valentine's Bind

that we could attend some with them, as their guests.

She went on to explain what was going on in the various scenes that were being played out in the back of the room in the dungeon. Pointing out the dungeon master she explained that he could step in and stop a scene if he thought it was necessary, but rarely did.

A waiter came over and we were both given soft drinks. Once again making me aware that tonight could be the second time I played in public for real.

Lily asked to use the bathroom and I was allowed to accompany her. Able to take a closer look at the various stations where people were playing. There was a male sub with a Dominatrix. He fastened to a cross naked being flogged.Sounding as if he was going to climax any moment until his Dominatrix reminded him not to. Which made me smile and I noticed Lily smiling too. I wasn't the only naughty sub by any means. It was nice to have a friend.

CHAPTER SEVENTEEN

Dariel

I watched petal as she disappeared to the bathroom, and my heart lurched.

Petal had no clue what I would ask of her tonight. Not an inkling. I would first of all, play with her in public, pushing her to the maximum extent of her limits.

If I was correct, and she managed to get past the fact that we were in a public place, giving me her absolute trust. Then the next step would be a given.

I was purposefully putting her into a situation that would test how well I had taught her. Also testing her belief in my ability to push her safely, without saying her safe word and stopping the scene.

At my signal the next step would go ahead. But would that signal happen. Who knew, but I was prepared and my friends knew of my intentions.

CHAPTER EIGHTEEN

Nicky

Sir and Simon were both stood when we returned, deep in conversation. They turned and greeted us both but didn't sit back down. Sir held out his hand and said just one word.

"Come"

"Yes Sir." I acknowledged.

Perhaps we were leaving I worried *So soon though?*

Then I realised where he was leading me. Toward the dungeon at the back of the room and people were gathering as if expecting a show.

Of course they were stupid and I would be one of the stars.

Strangely all the other scenes seemed to have stopped.

Funny that they all finished at the same time I thought.

I was led forward and positioned onto a spanking bench, pushed forward and secured.

Sir spoke to me calmly and clearly.

A Valentine's Bind

"Little one you remember the traffic light system of safe words? Please tell me in simple terms what they are and that you understand their meaning."

" Red is stop. Amber is "take a moment", and green is good to go. Sir." I said with a catch in my throat.

Oh Shit. I was going to play and everybody would be watching this time. Not just a few, but all of them.

I gulped at the thought of them all watching my Sir playing with me as I flushed crimson. My pussy weeping for joy.

He slid my thong down my legs, leaving me only in my corset and stockings. Stroking the skin on the inside of my thigh as he did and I shivered.

What was Sir going to do with me. What limit is he going to push here and now. I fretted

"You are such a good girl petal. Tonight I am going to push you to your limit on something we have discussed a few times, and you have seen what I will use. Do you remember the anal hook petal?"

I swallowed hard and replied. "Yes Sir I do."

"But first we will do some things I know you love. Okay?" He added.

"Thank you Sir. And Sir, I trust you implicitly and will do my best Sir" I responded.

He caressed and kneaded my bottom. Stroking towards my apex where my arousal was evident. The scent of my arousal so strong I could smell it myself. Then he began to spank me. At first they were fairly soft and gradually got harder. From one cheek to the other. Catching the sweet spot at the crease of my

A Valentine's Bind

arse. The sting quickly being replaced by heat and a throbbing. I moaned as it began to take effect.

Moving on to a pair of floggers he started out by dragging them across my body and my pussy. Then with a thud, the strength of his blows increased incrementally. The tingle and heat growing. The endorphins now beginning to take effect.

I began to make small noises. Moans and ahhs, oohs, unable to stay quiet as I gave voice to the pleasure I was experiencing.

He would stop and check the skin integrity soothing the pain and sending me higher as he occasional swiped through my drenched folds. Skirting my clit as his did but applying no pressure. He didn't need to I was getting more aroused with each blow and caress.

He came and stood in front of me, grabbed my hair and raised my head. Our eyes connected and I smiled.

"Oh petal your eyes tell me all I need to know. That, and your arousal. So responsive. So beautiful. Good girl petal. I am going to take time now as I insert the hook after I have plaited and bound your hair. What colour are you petal?"

"Green Sir ." I beamed.

He plaited my hair, then bound it. My anticipation rising once more. I was letting my Sir push me, and that mere fact had me more aroused than anything he did to me.

I felt his fingers then. Lubed and playing with my rosebud. Round and around driving me higher. He then pushed in and I relaxed as I was taught. A second finger joined the first. Stretching me ready. Something hard and cold now pushed against my anus and for a moment my attention slipped, but only a moment as Sir began to play with my folds. Up and down and around my clit.

Jesus I am going to cum if he keeps doing that. I thought. *Got to hold back or I will disappoint Sir.* My mind told me.

I managed to pull myself back from the edge. Biting my bottom lip so hard, I drew a little blood.

"Good girl. Push back now then relax how I taught you. I have got you petal. I always will have."

I pushed back and felt it enter.

"Ahhhh." I sighed

He tied the rope to the hook and I had to keep my head up now or it pushed deeper in response. He stood facing me again. Our eyes locked.

"Cum for me petal Come for your Sir." Her commanded

As he played with my nipples and applied pressure to my clit I screamed out my release. I knew he wouldn't stop. He said that he would make this memorable tonight. He did.

I pulled my head forward a little The hook travelling deeper in my arse as he sucked on my nipples and continued to circle my clit as once again I howled my release.

"Such a good girl petal. I am so proud of you, You amaze me every time we play." he marvelled.

As again I hit the heady heights of a climax. Screaming out as a huge third orgasm hit me like a

A Valentine's Bind

tsunami and I squirted over Sir's hands. When this began to ebb Sir started to remove the hook gently. Then the rope before I was released from the bench. My legs unable to hold me up as he effortlessly swept me into his arms. I placed my head on his shoulder. Unable to speak properly Muttering incoherently as he continued to stroke my hair.

He had me sat on his knee on the sofa.

I was deep in subspace. Away with the fairies as it were. In bliss. Powerless to move or respond just yet. Spent. I remember being given orange juice and some chocolate as I finally returned to earth.

I lifted my gaze to Sir and he said.

"Hello beautiful. I believe someone enjoyed that scene as much as I did. Maybe even more. Drink some more juice and eat this chocolate now."

He cuddled me close and stoked my hair.

Once I was recovered sufficiently Lily helped me go to the bathroom and brushed my hair for me. Smiling all the time.

"That was one of the best scenes I have ever witnessed Nicky. This life suits you."

CHAPTER NINETEEN

Nicky

As we walked out of the bathroom there was an air of expectation in the room and once again everyone was down near the dungeon.

Was someone else performing a scene? God I hope it's not for me again. Not sure I could manage another one tonight to be honest.

Lily led me forward and the circle opened and there was Sir.

Lilly pushed me forward toward him.

"Kneel sub." He instructed and as bidden I knelt into the waiting position. My heart thundering in my chest and my palms clammy.

Oh My God he is going to tell me he doesn't want me anymore. That our contract is over.

Tears gathered in my eyes.

He held in his hands a collar and I unconsciously reached up to touch mine. It was a different collar.

" Petal I offer you my collar. I offer you my Dominance. I offer to take you on a journey with me

A Valentine's Bind

and be my submissive. This is something I give willingly and with love. I will cherish, respect, protect and lead you. A bond greater than marriage. This is a lifetime commitment and not offered lightly. Do you accept my collar petal?"

I held my breath. *He loved me. Sir loved me and wanted me as his. I need to answer.*

I held up my hair, saying back to him.

" I accept your collar Sir. You already have my heart, soul and body. I now give it to you in front of others. I will proudly wear your collar and belong to you Sir." I responded joyfully.

His dimples showing as he moved forward. I lifted up my hair. He removed the red collar of consideration then gently fastened the new collar about my neck. The silver padlock locked in place, key on a cord that he placed around his neck.

I don't remember rising but in the next moment we were in each others arms.

Bound together for a lifetime.

A Valentine's bind.

A Valentine's Bind

A Valentine's Bind

A Valentine's Bind

AUTHOR INFO

I am passionate about writing, and write about passion. I am a qualified Children's Nurse, and have a degree and Pg Dip (Masters qualification), so probably not someone you would expect to write erotica. Although born in Salford I reside in Manchester, England. Although I gave up nursing in October 2014 in order to concentrate fully on writing. Love to read and write, but only started writing seriously in 2012. Music is important to me and this is why you are likely to find me attending gigs, and enjoying the Indie bands that abound in Manchester.

As an avid reader and writer I share reviews of books, gigs, album reviews and interviews on my blog.

I hope you enjoyed my book and I would love to hear form you.

A Valentine's Bind

You can find me on twitter @ScarlettFlame2
Facebook www.facebook.com/ScarlettFlame2
missscarlettflame.blogspot.co.uk
uk.pinterest.com/redgirl876/
ScarlettFlame.com

k

ALSO AVAILABLE

Also available

Bound For Passion
Erotic love stories

by

Scarlett Flame

Copyright © 2013 Scarlett Flame

When Vivienne sits inconsolable in the hospital chapel, the last encounter she expects is a fervent entanglement with an otherworldly being, as passions increase she learns for the first time in her life the true meaning of out of this world. In the second, Sarah meets a new lover after telling him all her intimate fantasies in an internet chat room. And, the final story concerns the journey a young woman takes, as a Dominant offers to show her the ropes, in exchange for her submission via BDSM. Individually these

A Valentine's Bind

stories are hot, but together they are sizzlingThe Visit

We had met on the internet. You know, in a chat room, and arranged to meet up.

The plane had just landed and I was extremely nervous, but excited. The things we had discussed online had made my heart race, so many fantasies that we had both had. Now that we were meeting up, maybe, hopefully, some of those fantasies would be fulfilled.

I stood waiting at the luggage carousel until I spotted my suitcase. The red satin ribbon I'd tied on the handle now seemed like a little flag.

I'd dressed in a slim fitting black pencil skirt, scarlet top and scarlet suede high heel shoes. My underwear was especially chosen with him in mind. A black lacy bra, a new black lacy thong, finished off with stockings and suspenders. A short black leather jacket over the top created the look.

Even when I'd retrieved my case, I loitered a few minutes longer by the carousel, wondering what would happen when we met. Would I even recognise him? We had seen pictures of each other, and he'd heard my voice. I knew he was over six foot tall, and he knew I was a little over five foot five inches, so he would be taller than me.

My hands were sweating a little now, and my legs were shaking too. Would I be able to go through with this? Would he? I nipped to the toilets, my nervousness making me need a pee. I brushed my hair and reapplied my make up, staring at my reflection.

A Valentine's Bind

I left the toilets, making my way slowly through the double doors in to the airport foyer, with my eyes firmly trained on my feet, worrying that I might trip, or fall, or do something stupid. Suddenly, I felt his gaze, and I just knew it was him. When I raised my head, and our eyes met, I spotted him straight away. There he was. Tall, dark, and handsome, and headed my way. It might have been cliché, but it was true, and he was mine, for the entire weekend.

My throat hurt now, and my heart stuttered in my chest. I stood stock still. As if my feet were suddenly encased in concrete, I couldn't move. He didn't falter, but instead gathered me up in his arms, then he was kissing me. A long, lingering kiss. The sort of kiss you never want to end. I dropped my bag and let go of my suitcase, oblivious to any one who may have been watching.

When he began to speak I detected the amazing Irish lilt I knew he would have and I just melted, well it felt that way to me. He picked up my suitcase and took my hand saying "I'm so glad you are here. My friend is going to drop us off at the hotel we are staying at. Come on, I can't wait for us to be alone."

We left the airport hand in hand and walked to the short stay car park. I could see a little white fiesta with a blonde haired guy in the driver's seat. Paul waved, and the guy got out and opened the boot. Paul put my suitcase in, next to a large holdall, and we both climbed in to the back of the car.

We sat there, not speaking, just holding hands, staring out of the window. The town was lovely and

4

quaint, with the houses painted all different colours, but my eyes kept drifting back to Paul. He began to speak immediately, "We're almost there now. This is Michael, by the way. We're meeting up with him and a few other friends later on tonight." Michael glanced over his shoulder at me and added "Hi, nice to meet you" Paul inched a little closer, our thighs touching now. I could feel the heat of his body through his jeans.

Michael pulled the car up to the front of a fairly nondescript hotel, called The Mermaid. Paul and I got out, he retrieved the suitcase and holdall, and we said our goodbyes to Michael.

As we walked in to the hotel, I began to think about the first fantasy we had discussed and could feel my face begin to flush. We approached the front desk and signed in, picking up our keys in the process. The Concierge enquired whether we needed some one to show us to our room. Paul replied, "No, thanks, we can manage," and we headed toward the lifts, opposite the desk. When he turned to me, his smile was more of a grin. "You ready to take the lift, Sarah?"

I gulped, and nodded. My mouth was too dry to speak now, as if it was full of sand. We got into the lift, and the doors closed with a whoosh.

Immediately Paul had me pinned against the side wall of the lift, indicating over his shoulder to the camera blinking in the corner. "You remember what we discussed?" Before I could respond he leaned in to me, kissing me deeply, ferociously. His hands wandered down toward the hem of my skirt and

A Valentine's Bind

continued their journey up the inside of my thigh.

By now my new thong was wet, as I remembered exactly what our "discussion" had been about. Discussion about a fantasy involving a lift, and what we would do there. With his free hand he pressed the "stop" button for the lift. Reaching his fingers into either side of my panties, he eased them slowly down, until he was knelt at my feet, and I was able to step out of them. He brought them up to his nose, sniffed deeply, and slipped them in to his jeans pocket, all the time making sure that the camera was recording everything. I was aroused, and embarrassed at the same time. Once again his hands travelled up the inside of my thigh. This time he inserted two fingers and gasped. "So wet, I knew you would love this. Just wait till we get to the room. I will rock your world."

Coming soon February 2016

The Prophecy Unfolds (Dragon Queen)

Life is not measured by the breaths you take, but by the moments that take your breath away - Anon.

For Alex, this was supposed to be a fresh start.
New job, new part of the country.
But she got much more than she bargained for.

A Valentine's Bind

As she travelled through the Snowdonian National park, with its remote villages and Wales' highest mountains, she stops to eat a bite of lunch.

There she is kidnapped by three strangers, and transported to the Dystopian, Steampunk world of Syros.

A world of dragons, magic and werewolves.

Where science fiction meets science fact.

This is only the beginning of an epic urban fantasy, and the fulfilment of a prophecy over 200 years old.

Will she survive on a planet where three factions battle for dominance.

Book One of the series Dragon Queen

Finally, my life was getting back on track following a worrisome number of months.

I had had a great deal of trouble sleeping lately as I had been continually disturbed by dreams I could only describe as nightmares!

These dreams always included the same shadowy characters with obscure faces. The one recurring theme, was that I became intimate with every one of them. To say this wasn't in my usual nature would be an understatement.

In all my relationships I had always been monogamous. Basically, I am a one man girl, and wouldn't dream of being unfaithful. Perhaps, because of this, these dreams proved highly disturbing and included sexual acts that I'd heard of, but would never think of participating in. I little suspected that

A Valentine's Bind

these dreams would prove to be the precursor to an amazing series of adventures

This story proper, began one day driving through the beautiful Welsh countryside on my way to check out some accommodation that I had secured. This was intended to act as a base to work from Monday to Friday, at my new job

Previously, I had been working in a general hospital close to my family home, but decided to spread my wings after ending a long term relationship with my childhood sweetheart, Paul.

I decided that I now needed some space to develop new friendships and to put my love life on the back burner. My career would become my first priority. So, this was part of that plan. I had taken a contract as a Children's Nurse for an Agency in a hospital situated near to Bangor in North Wales.

On that day I had been driving through the Snowdonia National Park, where pine trees crowded either side of the road. I had spotted a little picnic area to one side, flanked by a small car park. It was beautiful sunny day and as I had brought along a packed lunch. I decided to park up and take advantage of the glorious weather. I parked my car and then realised that mine was the only car, but thought no more about it. I had no problem eating here at the edge of the forest.

I retrieved my sandwich, carton of orange and the book I had just started and wandered over to the farthest table. From here I could watch the squirrels and birds as they searched amongst the bins for

A Valentine's Bind

crumbs.

I'd sat there enjoying my book for about ten minutes when two things happened. Firstly, I became aware that a hush had suddenly descended on the forest, and I could no longer hear the scampering of the squirrels or the birds singing. When I looked up I could no longer see any of them around the area they had occupied only a few minutes earlier.

The second thing was the sound I did hear. I can only compare that to the sound barrier being broken, a whoosh and a slight popping noise. Yet immediately after this, the birds and squirrels were back, chirping and moving through the grass once again.

I shrugged, went back to the page in my book and continued to eat. However, after a while a feeling of uneasiness descended on me. I raised my head to find myself being watched.

The watcher was a tall, broad -shouldered man with dirty blonde hair tied at the nape and he had the most vivid blue eyes I had ever seen. I estimated him to be about 25-30 years old. He was regarding me silently, and with intensity. His odd clothing caught my eye. Old fashioned garments, dark trousers laced up the front, a long-sleeved suede jacket of a similar material, and leather boots

I turned my head to look for any cars or vans on the car park, and jumped as I spotted two more men- one to my left and one I could see in my peripheral vision to the right. The man on the left was dressed similar to the first, but had sandy hair and sea green eyes.

In contrast he wasn't quite as broad, although

A Valentine's Bind

equally tall, (all three were over six foot tall.) The last had dark hair to his shoulders that hung loose, and the most amazing violet eyes.

The appearance of these men with no noise, and staring at me in rapt fascination, not uttering a word, spooked me. My heart was beating so loud and fast I thought that I was having some kind of heart attack.

But the most unnerving thing of all was all three men looked familiar, a deja vu sort of moment. I had dreamt about these three men for so long. I knew immediately these were the shady characters from my dreams. Dreams that repeatedly haunted my sleep.

I decided that sitting still was stupid, so made a grab for my bag and shot through to the right, I then ran toward one of the many footpaths I had spotted earlier.

My flight or fight response gave me swift feet, (or so I thought), but obviously not swift enough. Before I had got ten yards down the path two of the three had already moved, and appeared in front of me. They moved so fast I could hardly believe my eyes. I turned to head back to where I'd come from. Hoping I could make it back to my car.

Fate once again took charge, I turned and ran straight into the third man, the blonde. It was like running into a brick wall,as he ensnared me in his very muscular arms. My heart stuttered and I thought I felt the zing of an electric current run through my body. I never claimed to be a particularly brave person and I started to hyperventilate, gasping , trying to catch my breath.

A Valentine's Bind

One of them began to stroke my hair, saying "Calm down Alex, calm down. Breath slowly we won't hurt you" but, at that point my knees gave way and I collapsed into darkness, terrified. How did that man know my name was Alex?

When I came to I was lying on a huge bed in a strange bedroom – the biggest bed I'd ever seen, it was enormous! All I could think about was a little rhyme my granddad used to sing "Ten in the bed and the little one said roll over" it was so big! The other thing I immediately noticed, was how odd the lighting was. The lights looked like gas lamps of some sort but were giving off light. There were candles at either side of the bed too. How strange everything looked!

Sat on the bed next to me, to my right was the sandy haired man, on my left the dark haired man. Stood at the end of the bed was the blonde one. I looked agitatedly from one to the other and began to panic again. I was terrified and thought What did they want with me, and where was I? as I frantically tried to escape to the top of the bed, as far away as I could from my captors.

The sandy haired man handed me a glass of water but I was too frightened to drink it, What if it was drugged? I thought.

The blonde began to speak, his voice soft, but distinct. He introduced himself as Aston, pointed to the sandy haired man indicating that his name was Leon. Finally, nodding to my left and said "Vanda". Each in turn gave me a slight nod, but I still couldn't

A Valentine's Bind

respond.

Where the hell had they brought me to and why?
How on earth did they know my name was Alex and
they continued to stare, as if fascinated by what they
could see. my mind was chaotic.

I think Aston could see that I wasn't getting any
calmer but quite the reverse as I was now shaking so
violently my teeth had begun to chatter. He began to
speak again, slowly and clearly, in such a strange
accent I thought that he was European perhaps. Yet
his words were clear and concise.

"Alex, you need to calm down and sip some of the
water. We won't harm you. We could never harm you,
but quite the reverse. We intend to take care of you
and protect you from now on."

Oh oh, that was the wrong thing to say. Now, In
my head I was thinking What! and I thought that I
had been kidnapped by some foreign gang and about
to be abused by them all!! Not good at all!. I wildly
speculated.

Vanda then began to speak "Look at me Alex, look
at me"

I turned and looked into those beautiful violet eyes
and couldn't look away. I was mesmerised. It was
like I was set in stone, as I slowly began to relax and
began breathing more evenly. Yet I couldn't
comprehend why this was happening. I wanted to
look away, but my body wouldn't cooperate, and I
remained transfixed.

Aston spoke again. "We are not on your earth any
more Alex . We are on a planet called Syros in a

galaxy far from yours. Do you remember a strange popping noise ? Well, that was a portal opening from our planet to yours. It acts as kind of wormhole through space so that we can easily move from our universe to yours. We have been visiting your planet for millennia."